Dear parents,

*Math anxiety.* So many of us suffer from it. Yet every day we measure time or distance, look for patterns, estimate, and count. Whether we realize it or not, we are constantly thinking mathematically. And as parents we hope that our children will not succumb to our math prejudices.

We give children a great deal of encouragement when they are learning to count—but the encouragement needn't stop there. Young children love puzzles and riddles, and they eagerly approach problem-solving situations as if they were games. They often see and use a variety of strategies. These are important skills in developing mathematical thinking.

We truly have the power to nurture in our children a long-lasting love for math. We can do this by making a "math connection" to familiar experiences and by supporting our children's natural affinity for the discipline. **Step into Reading® + Math** books can help. Each book combines an age-appropriate math element with an enjoyable reading experience.

Remember—math is not an isolated phenomenon but is woven into the fabric of our lives. The love of math is a lifelong journey. Celebrate that journey with your child!

Colleen DeFoyd
Primary grades math teacher
Scottsdale, Arizona

*For my mom*
*—J.G.*

Random House 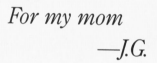 New York

Text copyright © 2000 by Julie Glass. Illustrations copyright © 2000 by Joy Allen.
All rights reserved under International and Pan-American Copyright Conventions.
Published in the United States by Random House, Inc., New York, and
simultaneously in Canada by Random House of Canada Limited, Toronto.

www.randomhouse.com/kids

*Library of Congress Cataloging-in-Publication Data*
Glass, Julie.
A dollar for Penny / by Julie Glass ; illustrated by Joy Allen.
  p.  cm. — (Step into reading + math. A step 1 book)
SUMMARY: Penny sets up a lemonade stand to earn money for
her mother's birthday card and learns about currency.
ISBN 0-679-88973-6 (pbk.). — ISBN 0-679-98973-0 (lib. bdg.)
[1. Money—Fiction.  2. Moneymaking projects—Fiction.
3. Birthdays—Fiction.  4. Stories in rhyme.]
I. Allen, Joy, ill.  II. Title.  III. Series: Step into reading + math. Step 1 book.
PZ8.3.G42635Do  2000  [E]—d21  97-31366

Printed in the United States of America  March 2000  10 9 8 7 6 5 4 3 2 1

Step into Reading® + Math

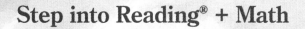

# A Dollar for Penny

By Dr. Julie Glass

Illustrated by Joy Allen

A Step 1 Book

In the shade,

I sell lemonade.

I have pink.

Stop and drink!

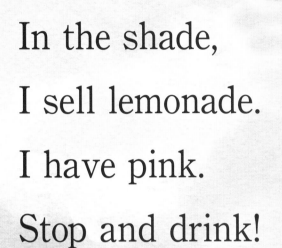

My aunt Jenny

pays one penny.

In my bank,

one penny goes CLANK.

The price goes up—
to two cents a cup!

Uncle Pete buys two.

Four cents is now due.

In my bank,

the pennies go CLANK!

The price goes up—

to five cents a cup!

Here are my cousins,
Kate and Lou.

They both want lemonade.

Woo-hoo!

Two nickels go CLANK
into my bank.

I have some lunch.
Munch, munch, munch.

For me,
the lemonade is free!

# The price goes up—
# to ten cents a cup!

Grandma Grime

pays a dime—

into my bank—

clink, clink, CLANK!

# The price goes up—
## to twenty-five cents a cup!

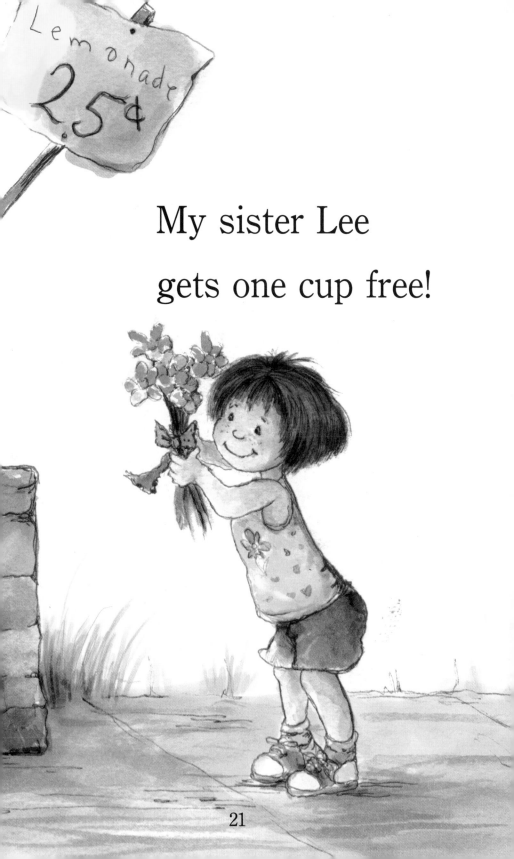

My sister Lee
gets one cup free!

My brother Sam

plays in a band.

He wants one cup.

He pays up.

In my bank,

one quarter goes

CLANK!

The price goes up—
to fifty cents a cup!
My dad buys one.
Selling lemonade is fun!

CLANK, clink, CLANK!
Two more quarters
in my bank.

# Time to count
# the total amount.

= 75¢

= 10¢

= 10¢

= 5¢

"Wow!" I holler.
"One hundred cents
is one dollar!"

I run to the store.

I look in the rack.

The card that I want

is way in the back.

It is red and green
and pink and blue.

Inside it says:

Happy Birthday, Mom.

I love you!

## 5 pennies          1 nickel

## 2 nickels          1 dime

## 2 dimes, 1 nickel          1 quarter

## 4 quarters          1 dollar